The Crocodile's knobbly Skin

Adapted from an original Namibian folklore tale

Retold by Andrea Florens

Illustrated by Claire Norden

Long, long ago in Africa, the Crocodile did not look as he does today. Was he knobbly and ugly? Oh no, the Crocodile was a very handsome creature. He was long and slim, and his soft and silky skin shone like pure gold.

Now because his skin was so silky and soft,
he had to take very good care not to damage it.
And because the sun shone so hot in Africa,
Crocodile knew he was never to leave
his muddy river during the day.

One evening the moon was
as big and round as it could be,
shining so brightly that nothing
was hidden by the night.
Crocodile lay on the bank of his muddy
river, his beautiful skin glowing like a
golden jewel in the moonlight.

It was not long before an owl flew past, and seeing this gleaming object, he stopped to take a look. Owl's big round eyes grew even wider. Never before had he seen such a handsome creature. He told the Crocodile just that, and then flew off to share the news with the other animals.

The news spread fast, and soon Cheetah, the fastest of all the animals, came to see Crocodile for himself. "Old Owl was right, you are the most magnificent creature in all the land! I myself am quite proud of my spots, but they're not a patch on your golden skin." Crocodile was very pleased.

Next Zebra came trotting down to the river. He too could not believe his eyes. "My stripes, I thought, were the most fashionable around. But your gleaming skin is by far the best I've ever seen!"

By now Crocodile was really enjoying this attention.

Soon many more animals were
crowded around him,
all ooohing and aaahing
over his splendid golden skin.
Crocodile was most pleased with all the comments,
and as he slipped back into the muddy water
before the sun came up, he told the animals to

visit him at the next full moon.

Under the muddy depths of the water,
Crocodile waited impatiently for the next full moon.
He had become vain and couldn't wait for all
the animals to admire him once more.
"A magnificent creature such as me
shouldn't have to hide away
for so long" he said to himself.

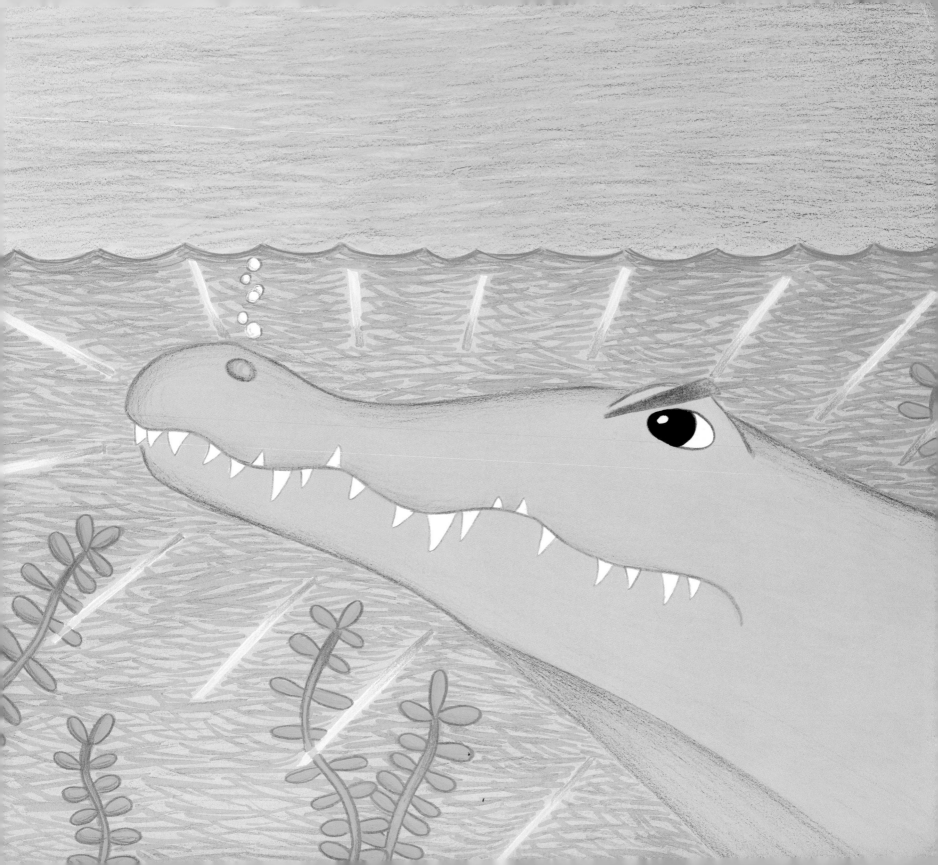

At last the days passed, and the moon shone bright and full. Crocodile climbed out onto the bank of the river once again. This time a crowd of animals were waiting to see him. The admiration was no disappointment. And by the end of the evening, Crocodile returned to the river, even vainer than before.

After a few days of waiting for the next full moon, Crocodile became very impatient.

Looking up at the sun
through the muddy waters,
he decided to lie on the bank of the river
for just a few minutes, so that the animals
could admire his magnificent skin.

And so that's exactly what he did.

First to find him lying in the sun
were a troop of monkeys.
And even they, who would usually make
fun of the other animals, were astounded
by Crocodile's beauty.

Then a flock of flamingos came
to see him. They were sure that the
beauty of their plumage, the colour of the pink
sunset on the clouds, could never be equalled. When
they saw the golden Crocodile, they stalked off in a huff.

Day after day Crocodile lay
on the bank of the river,
enjoying the admiration of the animals
who crowded around to see him.
So much did he like the attention, that he ignored
the sun that was beating down upon him.

But one day, when he climbed up out of the water,
he was not greeted with sweet ooohs and aaahs,
instead he heard unkind laughter.

A huge crowd of animals joined in
the laughter, pointing and jeering
rudely at Crocodile.

He looked down at his skin, and to his horror,
he saw what they were laughing at.

The harsh sun had turned his skin into **knobbly**, thick armour, no longer golden, but a hideous greenish-grey.

Crocodile dived as quickly as he could
into the depths of the water.
He never recovered from this humiliating experience.
And to this day he prefers to hide under the muddy water,

with just his eyes and his nostrils to be seen.

Published in South Africa by Art Publishers (Pty) Ltd
Reg. No 1947/027008/07
PO Box 334, Howard Place, Cape Town, 7045, South Africa
Tel: +27 21 532 3020
www.artpublishers.co.za

Second Revised Edition 2015